Zoya's
Journey

ISBN 978-1-0980-7967-3 (paperback)
ISBN 978-1-0980-7968-0 (digital)

Christian Faith Publishing, Inc.
832 Park Avenue
Meadville, PA 16335
www.christianfaithpublishing.com

Printed in the United States of America

Zoya's Journey

Tami Douglas

Little Zoya had a wonderful gift.
She only had to imagine it,
Speak it,
And so it became.

One very sunny day,
Zoya said to her mother,
"It will rain today."

Her mom says, "No, sweetie. It
is a beautiful sunny day.
There isn't one cloud in the clear blue skies."
Zoya repeated with certainty, "It will rain today."

You see, Zoya loved the rain.
She loved the smell.
And most of all, she loved to play in the puddles.

Zoya went to her room,
Took out her favorite yellow raincoat,
And her yellow rain boots.

Zoya got dressed and
sat on the porch
With her favorite bear.

Later that day, the skies became very cloudy.
Then the clouds got dark.
And behold, it began to rain.

Zoya ran outside
And danced in the rain.

"How did you know it would rain?" Mommy asked.
Zoya replied, "I didn't know. I just believed."

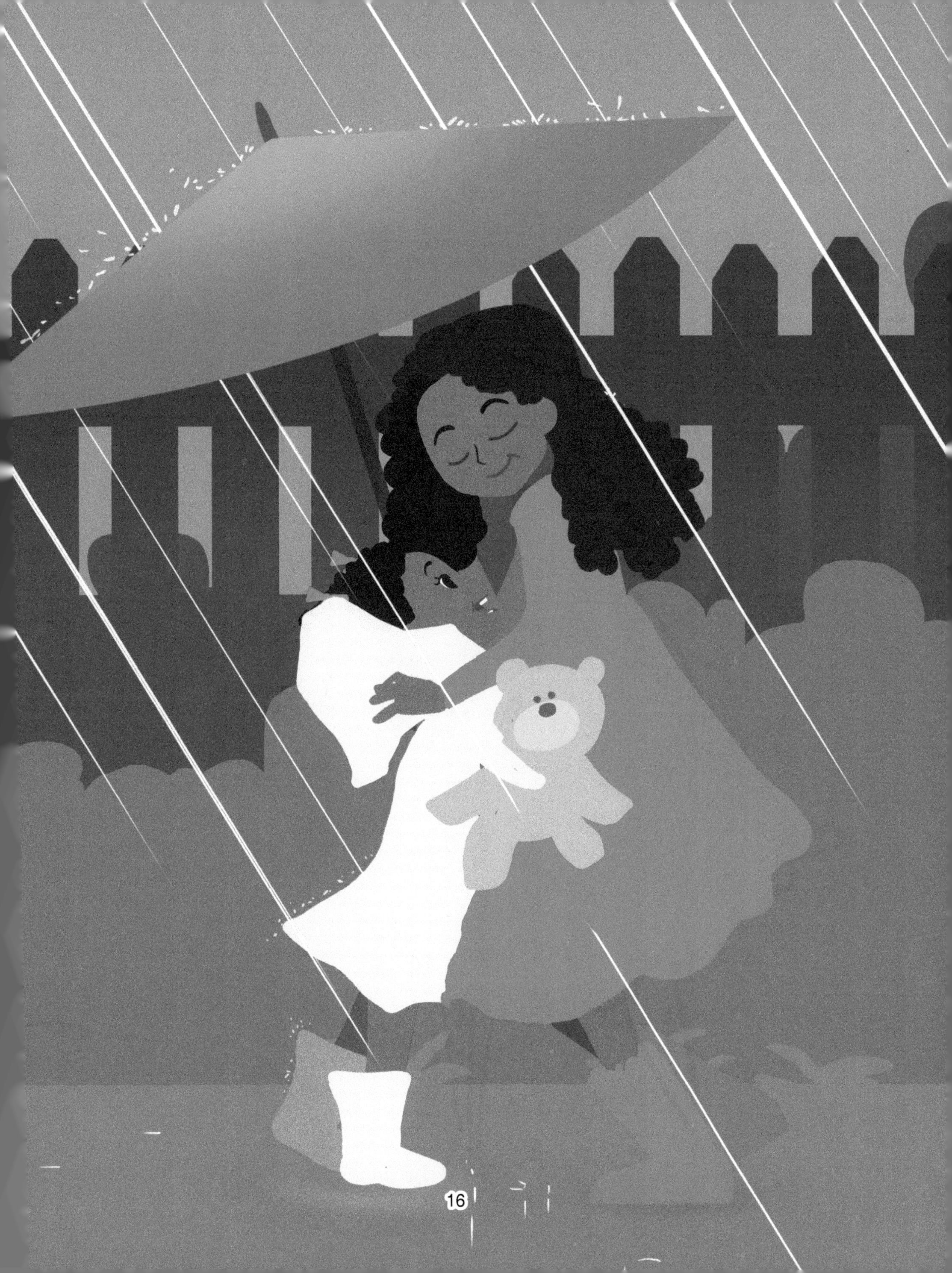

About the Author

Tami Douglas was born and raised in the tropical paradise of Jamaica but now braves the long, cold winters of Syracuse, New York. As a child, she always had her head in a book, escaping into the new realities that unfolded on paper.

Tami hopes to inspire children to believe in themselves by exploring life lessons of faith, love, and hope in her first of many books to come.

CPSIA information can be obtained
at www.ICGtesting.com
Printed in the USA
BVHW050939221121
622229BV00015B/557

9 781098 079673